New smells, new floors, new windows, new doors.
New garden, new porch...
Oh! So much to explore!

He walked from room to room,
and he noticed many things were just for him.
New bed, new dishes, and a basket full of toys!

"Hello, you little one!"
he heard a voice from above,
which made him look up.

And right there, on the window ledge,
was something strange.
A beautiful, silky blue cat
with big green eyes.

"My name is Aloof", she said,
jumping off the ledge and coming so close
as to touch his nose.

He didn't move, he didn't breathe,
he wasn't sure. He got scared but he didn't want
to let her know.

Urfy, Welcome to Your New Home!

A tiny cottage with large windows
overlooking a beautiful garden.

"From now on,
you're in charge of this entire land,
to watch and guard all creatures
small and large",
his mom said,
kissing him on his nose.

He felt overwhelmed.
He was only a puppy!
Will he find the courage?

A cat?
He had heard his sisters gossiping about cats...

...and not many good things!

"I heard you're in charge!" Aloof said.
"Yes, I am!" Urfy responded, lifting his head high.

"This is a wonderful place to run and explore.
Come! I show you around!"

He was amazed!
Aloof was nice, and not scary at all.
He thought of his sisters: They were all so wrong!

Aloof was small, and walked slowly,
just like him...
...but with so much grace!
She showed him the big garden.

"Oh! So many flowers and beautiful trees!" he said.
"Yes, and it's full of creatures.
Soon you'll discover!"

Aloof hadn't even finished saying that
when a family of rabbits hopped onto the path,
looking at him with curious eyes.

Then colorful ducks,
and a deer, a fox, and a flock of birds...
two owls, and some squirrels.

They were all talking at once!

"Silence! Urfy is only a puppy!
Give him time!"
Aloof commanded.

Urfy was amazed! Aloof was so small....
but she had so much courage!

Will he ever be like her?

Urfy settled quickly into his new home.

Each day he walked around
and explored the garden.

But most of all, he loved sitting by the
garden wall, between the flowers, watching
birds fly by. They were all in a hurry to build
their nests.

Everyone seemed busy,
passing by in a hurry, looking at him and shaking their heads.

No one believed he was up to the task,
to guard and protect.

Then, one evening, when he reached his
favorite spot...
someone was already sitting there!

And before he knew it, she ran so fast and
jumped right on top of him with such delight
that he couldn't help but join in her game!

They wrestled, rolled, and chased each other
with such joy!

And when they finally ran out of breath, they
collapsed laughing, next to each other,
by the wall.

"I'm Casey," she said. "I'm a golden retriever!"

"I'm Urfy," he answered."

"You look so different!" Casey wondered.
"I'm a collie!"

They looked at each other with clear curiosity.
They couldn't be more different!

She was so blonde, and he was so dark! She was
sturdily built, and he was more lean. Her ears were
short, but his were up. Her muzzle straight, and his
so long. But they both had wagging, feathery tails.

"Where did you come from?",
he asked her with curiosity.

"I live right there", she said,
pointing to a house that was on the other side of
the wall and across a vast field.
"Where do you live?"

"I live right here, in that cottage, and this is my
garden", he answered.

"Did you cross the field and jump over the wall?"
Urfy asked her. "Aren't you scared to venture so
far from home?"

"No!" Casey exclaimed.
"It's so much fun to explore! I have a big garden
with a big river where I can swim!"

"You!" he gasped. "Can you swim!?"
He was amazed.
"No, not yet!" Casey answered,
laughing while rolling on her back.

She was daring, fun, and very beautiful!

They sat together by the wall and talked about their homes, their sisters and brothers left behind, and their amazing new lives.

Together, hiding between the flowers, they watched the swallows... rather small birds, mostly dark in color but still with feathers that shined, with flashes of green and blue colors in the sun. All were working hard, carrying materials to build their nests.

Urfy was mesmerized by them,
but Casey had a better idea:

"Let's chase them!" she said.
"I bet I can catch one!"

She jumped up on her legs
and start running so fast!

She ran left, she ran right, she ran circles...

but no such luck to catch
a swallow in flight!

Urfy watched her from his spot.
He didn't follow her, and she didn't mind.

Casey came back to sit by him, her tongue
hanging and her fur all messed up!
She was a delight!

Then, they heard a voice in the distance calling, "Casey! Casey!"

"OH! I have to go now!" she said.

Casey climbed over the wall, but before she ran home she turned around, and looked at him with her big eyes.

"I'll see you tomorrow! Right here, by the wall!" And off she ran, just as fast as she could.

The next day, while walking down the lush garden path, he could hear a strange noise.

He stopped and listened....

He didn't like it at all. It was a knocking noise, coming from the trees.

How will he reach the wall?
He wanted to go back home, but he wanted to see Casey more.

Slowly he stepped forward,
but the knocking was louder and louder.

What could it be?

"He is afraid! He has no courage!"
he heard the mom fox saying to her cubs.

Urfy looked at them hiding between the tall grasses. Then, one little cub stepped on the path and came closer to him.

"Don't be afraid; it's the woodpecker family",
he explained.
"They live up in the trees that border the forest."

"I never saw a woodpecker before",
Urfy marveled.

"They are noisy little birds!"
the mother fox said, grabbing her
little cub before disappearing
into the tall grass.

Urfy listened again:
Knock! Knock! he could hear.
How strange!
But he had no more time to waste.
He rushed to meet Casey!

She was already there, sitting on the wall,
amusing herself with a butterfly.

As soon as she saw him, she jumped off the
wall and ran to him.

They rolled and wrestled and played with joy!
All felt so good; it was their joy.

Suddenly there was a loud scream, and the entire forest grew dark, covered by a black cloud!

Their ears went up, they sniffed the air, and they stood alarmed, not knowing what was there.

A few little colorful birds flew above them, and they could hear them talking about a young crow being trapped in a net!

Urfy looked up, trying to see above the trees... and what seemed to be a black cloud were hundreds of crows circling above the field.

"I have to go and help the crow", he said to Casey.
"But those crows look so scary!" she worried.

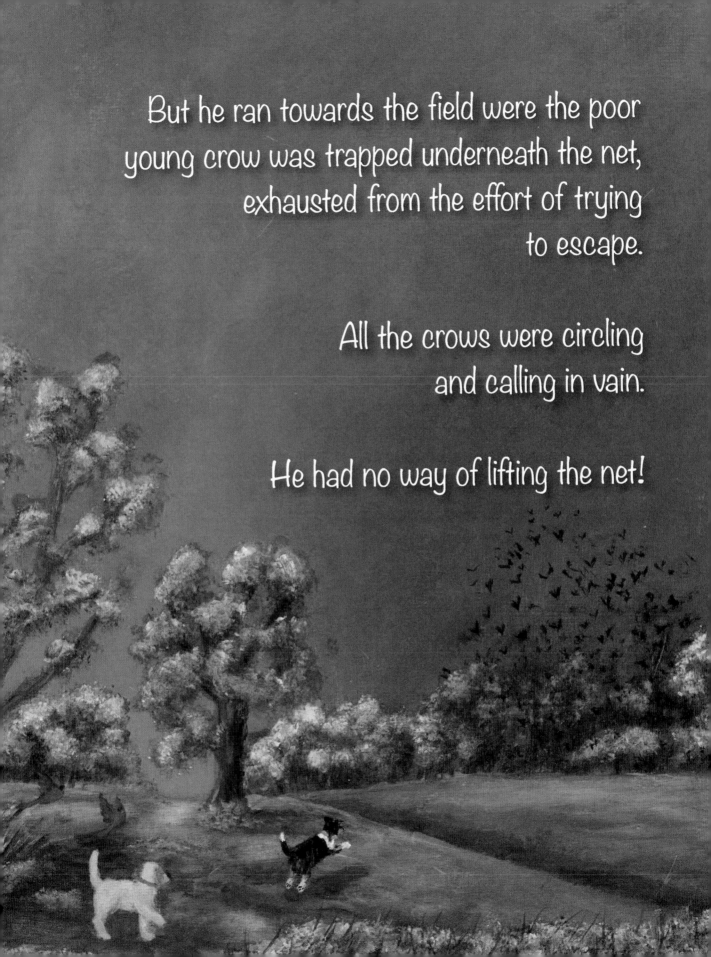

But he ran towards the field were the poor young crow was trapped underneath the net, exhausted from the effort of trying to escape.

All the crows were circling and calling in vain.

He had no way of lifting the net!

Urfy grabbed the net and started to pull.
And he pulled, and pulled...
but he wasn't strong enough.

He needed help!

He looked at Casey, and she understood!
They started to pull together until the little
crow was able to move.

The crow was free at last,
and everyone cheered!

"He has courage!"
.... "He saved the crow!"

Courage was hard, but he was able to do what he knew was right. And he finally understood his role in the land.

He felt confidence like never before. And all was clear.

He was a leader, a soul filled with compassion and kindness. He had a big heart that gave him courage and strength.

But most of all Casey was there for him; she was his best friend. Together they would guard and protect all creatures, small and large.

Aloof smiled.
She knew many wonderful things
will start to unfold now that a brave pure heart was
guarding their land.

Urfy and Casey playing "Catch me if you can!"

ISBN: 978-1-7340616-3-5 (paperback)
ISBN: 978–1-7340616-5-9 (ebook)

Illustrations by Denise Glova.
Book Design by Flora Scheck and Martin McDaid.